DATE DUE

F-Dy			
FE17'98			

DEMCO

RACHEL ISADORA

The Princess and the Frog

ADAPTED FROM
THE FROG KING AND IRON HEINRICH
BY THE BROTHERS GRIMM

GREENWILLOW BOOKS ◫ NEW YORK

Watercolor paints were used for the full-color art,
and pen-and-ink were used for the silhouettes.
The text type is Berkeley Old Style.

Printed in Hong Kong by South China Printing Co.

First Edition   10 9 8 7 6 5 4 3 2 1

Library of Congress Cataloging-in-Publication Data
Isadora, Rachel.
The princess and the frog/by Rachel Isadora.
p.   cm.
Summary: As payment for retrieving the
princess's ball, the frog exacts a promise
which the princess is reluctant to fulfill.
ISBN 0-688-06373-X.   ISBN 0-688-06374-8 (lib. bdg.)
[1. Fairy tales.   2. Folklore—Germany.]   I. Title.
PZ8.I84Fr   1989   398.2′1′0943—dc 19
[E]   88-61   CIP   AC

FOR JAMES

One day a young princess went walking in the woods that surrounded her father's palace. She came to a cool spring where she liked to sit. The princess had a golden ball in her hand. It was her favorite possession, and she amused herself by tossing it into the air again and again.

But once the princess threw the ball so high, it bounced
away and rolled right into the spring. She looked anxiously into
the water, but it was so deep she could not see to the bottom.
She began to cry and said, "If only I could have my ball again,
I would give all my fine clothes, my jewels—everything I have
in the world."

As the princess spoke, a frog popped his head up out of the water and said, "Princess, what makes you weep so bitterly?"

"My golden ball has fallen into the spring, but you nasty frog, what business is it of yours?"

"Perhaps I can help you," said the frog. "I don't need your fine clothes or jewels, but if you will let me be your friend and live in your palace and eat from your golden plate and sleep in your bed, I will bring back your ball."

What is that silly frog babbling about, thought the princess. Surely he can't leave the spring and live like a human being. Yet if I promise to do what he asks, he may get my ball for me.

"Very well," she said. "Just bring me my ball and I will do as you ask."

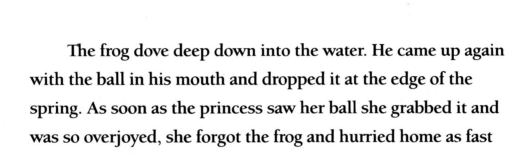

The frog dove deep down into the water. He came up again with the ball in his mouth and dropped it at the edge of the spring. As soon as the princess saw her ball she grabbed it and was so overjoyed, she forgot the frog and hurried home as fast as she could.

"Wait, Princess!" the frog called after her. "Take me with you as you promised!" But the princess did not stop.

The next day, just as the princess sat down to dinner, she heard a strange sound, *flip, flap, flip, flap,* as if someone were coming up the marble staircase.

Then there was a gentle knocking on the door, and a voice called, "Princess, young princess, open the door and let me in."

The princess ran to the door and opened it. There was the frog. She was so startled, she quickly closed the door and hurried back to the table.

The king noticed that the princess was upset and asked who was at the door. "It's a loathsome frog," she replied. "Yesterday he rescued my ball from the spring, and I promised him that he could be my friend and live with us here. But I never thought he would leave his spring."

"Princess, young princess," the frog's voice was heard again. "Let me in. Have you forgotten the promise you made to me yesterday?"

"Go and let the frog in," said the king. "You have made a promise, and you must keep it."

The princess did as she was told, and the frog hopped into the room and followed close on her heels to the table. "Now lift me onto your chair," he said, "so that I can sit next to you." As soon as she had done this, the frog said, "Now lift me up onto the table and push your plate closer to me so we can eat together," and the princess again had to do as she was asked.

When the frog had eaten his fill he said, "I am tired and would like to rest. Carry me upstairs and put me on your bed." The princess picked him up and took him to her room.

The princess placed the frog on her pillow, where he slept all night long. As soon as it was light he jumped up, hopped downstairs, and left the palace. At last, thought the princess, he is gone and won't bother me anymore.

But she was mistaken, for when night came again, the princess heard the same tapping on the door. When she opened it the frog came in, jumped onto her pillow, and slept until morning.

The third night the frog did the same, but when the princess awoke on the following morning she could not believe what she saw. Instead of a frog, a handsome prince stood at her side.

He explained how an evil fairy had bewitched him and changed him into a frog. The fairy had told him that he could regain his normal shape only if a princess would let him sleep in her bed for three successive nights.

The princess was delighted that it was she who had broken the spell, and the king invited the prince to be a guest in the palace. It was not long before the prince asked the princess to marry him and return with him to his father's kingdom. The princess gave her consent, and the marriage took place with great pomp and ceremony.

When the wedding was over, a splendid carriage arrived at the palace. It was drawn by eight white horses in golden harnesses, with white plumes on their heads. The prince and princess set out full of joy for the prince's kingdom, where they arrived safely and lived happily for many, many years.